· The *DISCOVERY of* ·
RAGONS
— *NEW RESEARCH REVEALED* —

For all the Dragons in my life – GB

Mr Greasebeam would like to extend his appreciation to his dear wife, and to the many and varied personages whose input has helped make this publication the wonderful creation that it undoubtedly is, most notably the highly esteemed Lesley Dunt, the long-suffering Cathy (Lars) Larsen and the ever-patient Roderick Davies Esq. without whom, etc, etc. Furthermore, with regard to this revised edition, Mr Greasebeam wishes to grudgingly acknowledge the valiant efforts of Michelle (it needs another comma) Madden, Jane (do you think so?) Godwin, Elizabeth (it looks okay to me) Dias and Splitting Image's indescribable Mick (what's a comma anyway?) Smith. Take the rest of the day off.

· The *DISCOVERY of* · DRAGONS

— *NEW RESEARCH REVEALED* —

Graeme Base

(a.k.a. Rowland W. Greasebeam, B.Sc.)

Abrams Books for Young Readers

NEW YORK

Cataloging-in-Publication Data has been applied for
and may be obtained from the Library of Congress.

ISBN 13: 978-0-8109-5967-5
ISBN 10: 0-8109-5967-4

Published in 2007 by Abrams Books for Young Readers, an imprint of Harry N. Abrams, Inc.
Original edition first published by Penguin Books Australia Ltd, 1996.
This revised edition first published by Penguin Group (Australia),
a division of Pearson Australia Group Pty Ltd, 2007

Author photograph by Robyn Base
Color reproduction by Splitting Image, Clayton, Victoria

Printed and bound in Singapore by Imago Productions F.E. Pte. Ltd.
10 9 8 7 6 5 4 3 2 1

HNA

harry n. abrams, inc.
a subsidiary of La Martinière Groupe
115 West 18th Street
New York, NY 10011
www.hnabooks.com

CONTENTS

INTRODUCTION

AN OVERVIEW OF SERPENTOLOGY

On the occasion of the Eleventh Anniversary Edition, 1908

IT IS ALL TOO COMMON, in this age of rising house prices and expensive overseas travel, for unscrupulous authors to attempt to boost lagging sales through the deplorable practice of publishing so-called 'Tenth Anniversary Editions'. I have steadfastly resisted the temptation to indulge in such tasteless acts of commercial self-interest, instead waiting until the eleventh anniversary to release this Fully Updated New Edition of my immensely readable and broadly informative book, *The Discovery of Dragons* (first published to critical acclaim in 1897).

Astute readers will note that there have been absolutely no changes made to the original text of the book. This is due to the fact that it was completely perfect in every way. However, those same readers will be delighted and amazed by the addition of a brand-new chapter revealing a whole new Serpentological genus: the New World Dragon.

Whilst certain members of the scientific community are still determined to oppose me (and I note with sadness that my one-time colleague, Marty Fibblewitz, continues, even after all these years, to side with the doubters), I remain resolute that the letters available to me ten years ago (whoops, eleven) documenting the first Human-Dragon interactions prove that the discovery of Dragons can be rightly credited to three historical figures – Bjorn of Bromme, a ninth-century Viking; Soong Mei Ying, youngest daughter of an obscure thirteenth-century Chinese silk trader; and Dr E. F. Liebermann, an even-more-obscure nineteenth-century Prussian cartographer and amphibiologist.

However, it is with great pride, and modest expectations of significant personal gain, that I now introduce to the world of Serpentology a new name: Francisco de Nuevo. The fact that you must buy a whole new book in order to find out about him (unless you are one of those despicable people who read books then put them back on the shelf) is not my fault.

Prof. Rowland W. Greasebeam, B.Sc. (Serp.)
F.R.Aud. (Melb.)
Editor
Melbourne

CHAPTER ONE

The Discovery of
EUROPEAN DRAGONS

The Letters of Bjorn of Bromme

With its leathery hide and distinctive flared nostrils, the European Dragon is to many people the very essence of Dragonhood. However, the widely held belief that all European Dragons belch fire and smoke is incorrect. The only true pyroprojectile Dragon in this group is the Emerald Dragon of Ireland (see page 6). The Great Snow Dragon of Greenland often mimics the effect by releasing quantities of superheated steam into the frozen Arctic air, creating a sparkling cloud of phosphorescent gas, and the Welsh Red has been known to smoulder on occasions, but neither is a true fire-breather.

WHEN BJORN OF BROMME first set sail from his fjord-ringed homeland towards Ancient Britain, his thoughts were of looting and pillaging, as was generally the case with ninth-century Vikings. But this remarkable man was destined to become far more than just a simple-minded, lice-infested Nordic Barbarian. In the words of 'Professor' Marty Fibblewitz: 'If you ask me, this Bjorn of Bromme fellow was a complete and utter . . .' genius. (And this from a man who has since found it necessary to ridicule me and my ideas at every opportunity, presumably because he knows his own feeble efforts at getting published will only result in a garage full of books that no one wants to buy, whilst *my* work is even now being closely considered for *reprinting*. So there!)

In the letters that follow it will become clear that Bjorn of Bromme can rightly be credited with the discovery of the four main species of European Dragon. (The only possible exception is the St George Dragon, first noted by Bjorn's fellow-seafarer Sigurd of Sveden; however, it can be argued that Sigurd would never have been in Spain in the first place if not for the navigational skills of his famed captain, so I like to think that Bjorn can, to some extent, take credit for this discovery as well.)

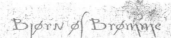
Bjørn of Bromme
VIKING
General Looting and Pillaging ※ Gratuitous Violence a Speciality ※ No Job Too Small
1a Westfjord Road, Valhalla Meadows, Norway

To: Ølaf the Grim
33 Viking Way, Valhalla Meadows, Norway

Greenland
6th April, A.D. 856

Dear Ølaf,

Bad news, I'm afraid. Got lost on the way to Britain and have ended up in a barren land completely covered in snow and ice. Thought I'd call it Greenland. Sorry about the mix-up. Hope the looting and pillaging went well.

The wildlife here is a bit startling, I can tell you. The boys and I went out hunting for something to eat last week and a blizzard blew up — couldn't see a thing. All of a sudden these three huge bird-lizard-monster things came rushing out of the snow, screeching and flapping their wings. Looked just like those big, ugly carvings we've got on the pointy end of our ships to scare the Ancient Britons with. What is it they're called again? — nogyns or drogyns or something? Dragyns? Anyway, scared me half to death they did. Poor Sven didn't stand a chance.

The rest of us will be heading home soon, but I thought we'd just have a quick look around first — see what else turns up. Should be back in time for the Midsummer Rampage.

Fond regards,

Your affectionate cousin, Bjorn of Bromme

P.S. Called the new discovery the Great Sven-eating Dragyn* on account of how poor old Sven got eaten and all. Actually I've been wondering where Lars has got to over the last couple of days. Maybe there's a Great Lars-eating Dragyn around too? I'll let you know.

* Subsequently renamed the Great Snow Dragon – Editor.

PLATE 1: GREAT SNOW DRAGON   Pictured here very much as Bjorn of Bromme must have first seen them, three Great Snow Dragons emerge screeching from a swirling Arctic tempest in search of unsuspecting Nordic riff-raff. Note the clouds of superheated steam issuing from their nostrils.

Bjørn of Brømme
VIKING AND EXPLORER
Experienced in Dragyn Wørk
c/o 1a Westfjørd Road, Valhalla Meadows, Norway

To: Ølaf the Disagreeable   Ireland
33 Viking Way, Valhalla Meadows, Norway   23rd June, A.D. 856

Dear Ølaf,

      I was wrong about the Lars-eating Dragyn; it was the Great Sven-eating Dragyn again. Looks like I'll have to change its name to the Great Sven-and-Lars-eating Dragyn. Ør should I just settle for the shorter Bjorn's Viking-eating Dragyn and be done with it? Making decisions like this is all part of being a Great Explorer, you know.

      Sorry to hear the raid was a bit of a flop, but I don't see how it was all my fault. I can't help it if the Ancient Britons are onto us and have moved inland. Frankly I think the bottom is falling out of the whole Viking business and we should look at reindeer farming or something instead.

      Anyway, after Lars got eaten I decided to set sail for home, but things just haven't worked out from a navigational standpoint on this trip. We sailed due east for three weeks, then headed northward, expecting to hit the coast somewhere near the Happy Horns Health Club — the boys hoped we might even stop in for a sauna — but somehow we've ended up in a place called Ireland. I think you might have to start the Rampage without us.

      Interesting news on the Dragyn front, however. The other day Dagbar and I were stuck in a bog when a beautiful green Dragyn came gliding down out of the sky. It was about the size of a small horse. Dagbar thought we should call it the Small-horse-sized Dragyn, but I told him not to be so stupid. That was just before it carried him away. I've named it the Great Dagbar-eating Dragyn for obvious reasons.*

Slainte! Bjorn

Renamed the Emerald Dragon in recent years — Editor.

PLATE 2: EMERALD DRAGON (IMMATURE)   Up to the age of 13 the young Emerald Dragon is vulnerable to attack from a range of stinging insects due to its fragile, almost translucent skin. However, as the Dragon matures, its pyro-projectile ability emerges as an effective deterrent to most adversaries. In this scene an ill-advised Kokinos Bee zeros in on an adolescent Dragon, unaware of its imminent demise.

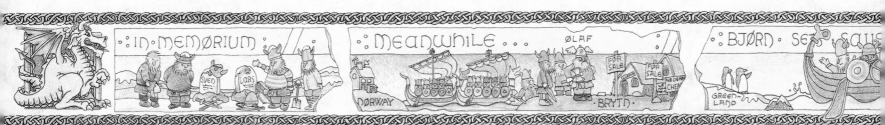

Bjørn
THE DRAGYN MAN
For All Your Dragyn-related Needs
Inquiries: P.Ø. Bøx 2, Valhalla Meadøws, Nørway

To: Ølaf the Extremely Bad-tempered
    33 Viking Way, Valhalla Meadows, Norway

Britain S.W.2
9th May, A.D. 857

Dear Ølaf,

Thanks for yours of 7th Jan '57. I really do think you're getting this all out of proportion — I realise you need the boat for other voyages of destruction, but I'm sure we'll be back well before the First Raid of the New Year. At least we've finally made it to Britain, though looting and pillaging seem to be out of the question. Anyway, all our swords and clubs are back in Ireland — they sank in the bog like poor old Cenn and Bryn. Did I tell you about them last time? That left just Sigurd, Jorgen and me.

The good news is I've found another Dragyn. Beginning to think I've got a real knack for this line of work! We were off on a bit of a jaunt (Sigurd had been thinking about maybe burning a village or two further up the coast for old time's sake) when we were hit by a terrible smell coming from a cave in a cliff high above us. I sent Jorgen up to investigate. He was a good man, poor Jorgen — but a bit clumsy when it came to climbing, as it turned out.

Sigurd and me waited until the Welsh Red Dragyn* what lived in the cave (I've called it that on account of it being Welsh and red) had finished with Jorgen, then we crept up for a quick look inside. The cave was full of armour and swords — fabulous riches — but somehow I felt they were best left alone. Let sleeping Dragyns lie, I say; especially this ugly brute.

I know you're not going to be too pleased about this, Ølaf, but me and Sigurd thought we might just pop down to Portugal or Spain since we're over this way — catch some rays, then head across to the south of Gaul for the summer. Good luck with the Rampage. I'll be thinking of you.

Cheers, Bjorn

* The name Welsh Red Dragon was actually quite appropriate and has remained until the present day – Editor.

PLATE 3: WELSH RED DRAGON   An uncompromisingly bad-tempered brute, the Welsh Red is a compulsive hoarder, often of useless things like old prams or six-month-old computers, but sometimes of genuine treasures such as gold, jewellery or out-of-print Australian children's books.

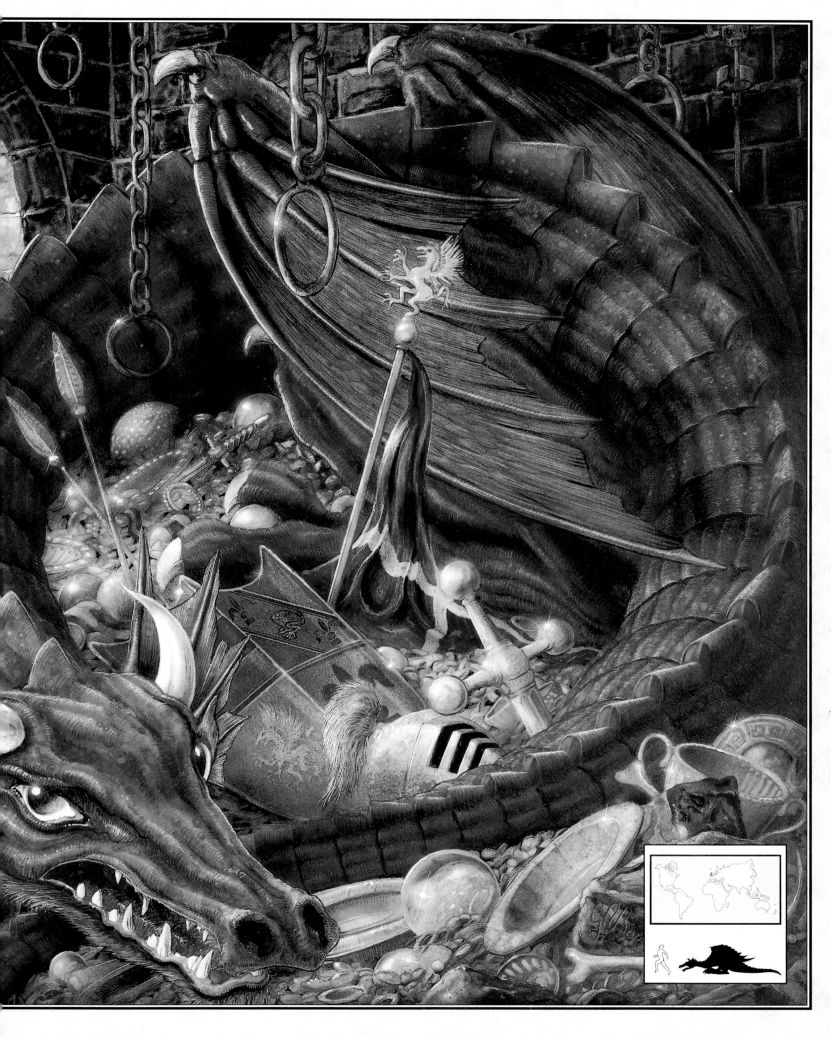

Bjørn the Great

DRAGYNSLAYER (RETIRED)
Dragynløre Expert and Championship Beach-vølleyball Expønent
'Maisøn de Bjørn', 879 Rue Sølaire, Très Nice, Gaul

To: Ølaf the Glum and Resigned
Manager, Rødsnute Reindeer Farm
Hammerfest, Norway

South of Gaul
1st May, A.D. 863

Dear Ølaf,

How are things in freezing Norway? Glad to hear the reindeer business is working out. Sorry I missed the First Round-up, but the beaches down here are just sensational.

Sigurd's taken over the role of Great Explorer now – I've gone into retirement. Thinking of maybe publishing a book about my adventures. I'm going to call it 'Bjorn – DragynSlayer'. Has a good commercial ring to it, don't you think?

I heard Sigurd discovered a Dragyn in northern Spain a year or so ago – a really big one with lots of teeth, and rows of precious stones all down its sides.* Sigurd has decided to stay on in Spain indefinitely. Well, I assume he's staying on, seeing as he's inside the Dragyn now. He always was a one for precious stones, was old Sigurd.

Anyway, must fly; the finals of the beach-volleyball competition start in an hour or so and I've just got time for a quick dip first.

Au revoir,

Your relaxed and tanned cousin, Bjorn

Sigurd the Svede named his discovery the Great Big Dragyn with Lots of Sharp Teeth and Heaps of Precious Stones; however, in the late Middle Ages, when it was identified as the Dragon that had the famous run-in with St George of England, its name was changed accordingly – Editor.

PLATE 4: ST GEORGE DRAGON   Much maligned for the unpleasant business concerning St George of England, the St George Dragon is in fact a gentle giant, more at ease with a pile of cabbages than a knight on horseback. Whilst younger, more boisterous members of the species may be tempted to indulge in a juicy portion of peasant every now and then, mature St George Dragons are almost entirely vegetarian and can most commonly be seen in the remoter parts of Andalucia, lying in wait for passing grocery trucks.

MONGOLIAN
SCREAMERS

JAPA
BUTTE
LIZA

EAS
TE
WO

CHAPTER TWO

The Discovery of
ASIATIC DRAGONS

The Letters of Soong Mei Ying

The classic Asiatic Dragon is a ferocious and cunning beast that has earned a special place in the hearts and minds of the multitudinous peoples of Asia. Not surprising really: anything that's planning ways to have you for breakfast deserves a little respect, if you ask me. Strange, then, that these magnificent animals should not have been discovered until the late thirteenth century, and then by a diminutive young woman who had no prior experience in Serpentology whatsoever. But such is the case, as the following letters will demonstrate. No doubt 'Professor' Smartypants Fibblewitz would disagree, but then this is the man who would have us believe Dragons evolved on one of the moons of Jupiter and were brought to Earth by the Aztecs, so I think we can disregard his opinions as no more than the product of a feeble mind, thank you very much.

IN 1277, SOONG MEI YING, daughter of a thirteenth-century Chinese silk trader, set out from the imperial city of Ch'ang-an with a bundle of silks, hoping to earn sufficient money in the markets of distant Kathmandu to pay the growing medical bills of her gravely ill father. At a narrow mountain pass her caravan was waylaid by a pair of marauding Mongolian Screamers, and Mei Ying lost all her wares. In despair she started back towards Ch'ang-an but along the way discovered a creature whose value made her precious silks look like worthless rags: the fabulous, mythical Japanese Butterfly Lizard.

From this beginning, Soong Mei Ying embarked upon an adventure that was to change the face of Serpentology forever . . .

13TH FEBRUARY, 1277

FOR THE GRACIOUS ATTENTION OF:
SOONG CHEN YI
76 FLOPPY WILLOW BOULEVARD
CH'ANG-AN

DEAR FATHER,

FORGIVE MY DISOBEDIENCE. I HAVE LEFT CH'ANG-AN DESPITE YOUR FORBIDDING ME TO DO SO, BUT MY ACTIONS, HOWEVER FOOLISH, WERE DICTATED SOLELY BY MY LOVE FOR YOU, DEAR FATHER. HOW COULD A DUTIFUL DAUGHTER HAVE STOOD BY WHILE THAT INCOMPETENT PHYSICIAN LAU ZHANG FU LINED HIS POCKETS WITH GOLD AT HER AILING FATHER'S EXPENSE? I THEREFORE CONCEIVED OF A MOST AUDACIOUS PLAN - WHICH IS CERTAIN TO SURPRISE YOU, FATHER, SINCE YOU KNOW ME TO BE BUT A TIMID THING, SCARCELY CAPABLE OF BOLD ACTIONS.

I TOOK A BUNDLE OF FINEST SILKS FROM THE FAMILY WAREHOUSE, INTENDING TO SELL THEM AT THE GREAT MARKETS OF DISTANT KATHMANDU: THE MONEY WOULD HAVE BEEN SUFFICIENT TO PAY OFF LAU ZHANG FU AND EMPLOY A REAL DOCTOR TO CURE YOUR DEBILITATING AILMENT. HOW MY HANDS TREMBLED AS I LEAPT THE WALL OF THE WAREHOUSE, ELUDED THE GUARDS, FORCED THE DOOR AND MADE OFF SILENTLY WITH THE PRECIOUS PACKAGE!

BUT, ALAS, MY PLANS NOW LIE IN RUINS. THE CARAVAN WITH WHICH I LEFT CH'ANG-AN - HAVING FIRST DISGUISED MYSELF AS A SIMPLE PEASANT GIRL - WAS WAYLAID IN A NARROW MOUNTAIN PASS BY A PAIR OF MARAUDING DRAGONS: FEARSOME BEASTS WITH EVIL TONGUES AND VICIOUS DISPOSITIONS.* I HAD THOUGHT SUCH CREATURES EXISTED ONLY IN MYTH!

WHEN THE TERRIBLE BEASTS DESCENDED UPON OUR CAMP, SCREECHING AND FOULING THE AIR WITH THEIR APPALLING STENCH, I WAS FILLED WITH FEAR AND LOATHING. BUT, MOMENTARILY OVERCOMING MY NATURAL TIMIDITY - FOR I AM OF COURSE ONLY A WEAK THING MORE USED TO NEEDLEPOINT THAN FIGHTING DRAGONS - I GRASPED A FLAMING BRAND FROM THE FIRE AND LEAPT FORWARD TO DRIVE THEM OFF. MY FELLOW-TRAVELLERS MEANWHILE FLED INTO THE WOODS. NO DOUBT THEY WERE ATTEMPTING TO LURE THE DRAGONS AWAY, SO I MUST NOT ALLOW MYSELF TO ENTERTAIN THE NOTION THAT THEY DISPLAYED LESS FORTITUDE THAN FRIGHTENED RABBITS.

DESPITE MY EFFORTS, THE HIDEOUS BEASTS EVENTUALLY PREVAILED (THOUGH I HAVE HOPES THAT ONE DRAGON AT LEAST RECEIVED A MORTAL BLOW). I WAS UNHURT, BUT DEVASTATED TO FIND THE PRECIOUS SILKS ENTIRELY RUINED.

I HAVE DISOBEYED YOU, MY BELOVED FATHER, AND THROUGH MY FOOLHARDY ACTIONS CAUSED GREAT LOSS TO OUR FAMILY FORTUNES. I SHALL RETURN TO CH'ANG-AN FORTHWITH, IN THE MOST DEJECTED OF SPIRITS.

YOUR FAITHFUL DAUGHTER,

MEI YING

The Mongolian Screamer was in fact quite common in that part of the world in the thirteenth century, but until Soong Mei Ying's encounter no one had survived to report its existence – Editor.

PLATE 5: MONGOLIAN SCREAMER   Ever since the discovery of the Mongolian Screamer, its complex and extremely anti-social linguistic abilities have fascinated serpentologists the world over. It is credited with no less than seventy-three distinctive calls, all of which appear to be either openly aggressive or offensive to other Dragons.

24TH APRIL, 1277

FOR THE GRACIOUS ATTENTION OF:
SOONG CHEN YI
76 FLOPPY WILLOW BOULEVARD
CH'ANG-AN

DEAR FATHER,

WONDERFUL NEWS! I HAVE MADE AN EXCITING DISCOVERY THAT I BELIEVE HAS THE POTENTIAL TO FREE YOU FROM THE DISCOMFORT OF YOUR DISTRESSING AND PROTRACTED AILMENT - AND MAY ALSO GO SOME WAY TOWARDS DEFLECTING ANY PATERNAL ANGER CONCERNING CERTAIN RUINED SILKS!

AS I JOURNEYED BACK TOWARDS CH'ANG-AN, DOWNCAST AND FORLORN, I TURNED ASIDE AT A ROADSIDE SHRINE TO LIGHTEN THE HEAVY BURDEN OF SADNESS THAT LAY UPON MY SOUL (AND THE HEAVY BURDEN OF WEARINESS THAT LAY UPON MY FEET). IN THE GARDEN OF THAT RESTFUL PLACE MY CONTEMPLATIONS WERE INTERRUPTED BY THE SLIGHTEST OF SOUNDS: A SOFT THRUMMING, COMING FROM JUST ABOVE MY HEAD. I LOOKED UP TO SEE AN EXQUISITE DRAGON, SCARCELY LARGER THAN A SONGBIRD, DRAWING NECTAR FROM THE CHERRY BLOSSOMS.

AT ONCE MY HEART LEAPT FOR I RECALLED A PASSAGE IN THE CHRONICLES OF THE ANCIENT SAGES THAT DESCRIBED A MAGICAL CREATURE, LIGHT OF BODY AND WITH THE FINEST OF GOSSAMER WINGS. THE CREATURE WAS SAID TO POSSESS HEALING POWERS BEYOND THOSE OF EVEN THE WISEST OF PHYSICIANS. FATHER, I HAVE FOUND THE MYTHICAL BUTTERFLY LIZARD OF ANCIENT JAPAN!*

THE CREATURE WAS ALARMED BY MY PRESENCE AND AT ONCE TOOK TO THE AIR, BUT I SOOTHED IT BY SOFTLY PLAYING MY LUTE. (HOW THANKFUL I WAS THAT MY CLEVER FATHER HAD INSISTED I PERSEVERE WITH MUSIC PRACTICE, DESPITE CONTINUAL OBJECTIONS FROM MYSELF, THE NEIGHBOURS AND MOST OF THE LOCAL DOGS.) TO MY JOY THE CREATURE CAME TO ME, WONDROUSLY UNAFRAID, AND ALIGHTED UPON MY OUTSTRETCHED ARM. EVEN NOW IT IS SAFELY CONCEALED WITHIN THE FOLDS OF MY TUNIC AS I RETURN HOME WITH ALL SPEED, IN THE FERVENT HOPE THAT I MAY HAVE FOUND THE ANSWER TO YOUR MALADY.

YOUR FAITHFUL (IF SOMEWHAT UNDISCIPLINED) DAUGHTER,

MEI YING

A creature fitting the description of the Japanese Butterfly Lizard is mentioned in a fanciful ballad written by the Japanese sage and songster Karioke in A.D. 342. The popular number 'I Left My Harp in Sampan Disco' contains a dream sequence in which the composer speaks of a magical creature that healed his broken heart – Editor.

PLATE 6: JAPANESE BUTTERFLY LIZARD These diminutive Dragons secrete a sweet-scented oil from glands beneath their wings. The healing properties of this oil defy medical explanation; however, the oil appears effective in the treatment of a wide range of ailments.

1ST JUNE, 1277

FOR THE GRACIOUS ATTENTION OF:
SOONG CHEN YI
76 FLOPPY WILLOW BOULEVARD
CH'ANG-AN

DEAR FATHER,

ALAS, MY RETURN TO CH'ANG-AN HAS BEEN DELAYED. FIVE NIGHTS AGO A FIERCE STORM FORCED ME TO SEEK SHELTER IN A SQUALID TAVERN FREQUENTED BY BRIGANDS, SWINDLERS AND USED-RICKSHAW DEALERS. TO MY DISMAY THE JAPANESE BUTTERFLY LIZARD WAS TAKEN FROM ME AS I SLEPT.

UPON AWAKENING AND REALISING MY GREAT LOSS, I IMMEDIATELY SET OUT TO TRACK THE THIEVES DOWN. THEIR TRAIL WAS CLEAR IN THE OVERNIGHT SNOW – I GUESSED THEY WERE PERHAPS FIVE IN NUMBER – AND I FOLLOWED AFTER THEM, DAY AND NIGHT, UNTIL I REACHED THE GATES OF A GREAT TEMPLE. BUT HERE THE TRAIL ENDED. THE TEMPLE ITSELF WAS DESERTED, AND I SOON REALISED WHY: A PAIR OF HUGE AND EVIL WINGED CREATURES HAD MADE THEIR NEST IN THE TEMPLE FORECOURT. TWO OF THE BANDITS LAY DEAD WHERE THEY HAD ENCOUNTERED THE TERRIBLE BEASTS, BUT THE REMAINING THIEVES AND THE PRECIOUS JAPANESE BUTTERFLY LIZARD WERE NOWHERE TO BE SEEN.

I OBSERVED THE HORRID CREATURES FROM THE SAFETY OF AN OVERHANGING BRANCH AND WAS REMINDED OF THE MANY CARVED STATUES OF MYTHICAL WINGED WORMS THAT STAND IN THE PARKS AND GARDENS OF CH'ANG-AN. I HAVE THUS CHOSEN TO CALL THIS NEW DISCOVERY THE COMMON GARDEN WORM.*

WHILE I WATCHED AND CONSIDERED HOW BEST TO DRIVE THE WORMS FROM THE TEMPLE, I SUDDENLY HEARD A SOFT THRUMMING AND KNEW THE JAPANESE BUTTERFLY LIZARD MUST BE AT HAND. I SPIED THE CREATURE PERCHED AT THE FAR END OF MY BRANCH AND EDGED OUT TO RETRIEVE IT. BUT THE BRANCH WAS ROTTEN AND, EVEN AS MY HAND CLOSED AROUND THE LIZARD, I FELL TO THE COURTYARD BELOW! HOW THANKFUL I WAS TO HAVE LEARNT SOME SIMPLE ACROBATICS BY WATCHING MY HONOURED FATHER PRACTISING THAT ANCIENT SKILL WHEN I SHOULD HAVE BEEN CONCENTRATING ON MY NEEDLEPOINT. FOR THUS I WAS ABLE TO FALL IN SUCH A WAY AS TO DAMAGE NEITHER MYSELF NOR THE PRECIOUS DRAGON.

THE WORMS IMMEDIATELY CAME AT ME, BUT THEY WERE SLOW AND LETHARGIC, AS IF WEIGHED DOWN BY A LARGE AND RECENT MEAL. I REALISED THEN WHAT HAD BECOME OF THE OTHER THIEVES. I DEPARTED THE TEMPLE WITHOUT DELAY, AND AM NOW ONCE MORE ON MY WAY HOME. THE LEGENDARY BUTTERFLY LIZARD OF JAPAN WILL SOON BE IN CH'ANG-AN.

YOUR FAITHFUL DAUGHTER,

MEI YING

---

* *The statues in the gardens of Ch'ang-an were subsequently found to resemble more closely the Red-bellied Hooter, an extremely territorial and bad-tempered species of Worm discovered by Soong Mei Ying some years later. As a result the Common Garden Worm was renamed the Eastern Temple Worm – Editor.*

PLATE 7: EASTERN TEMPLE WORM   The propensity of Asiatic Worms to 'adopt' temples is well documented. However, this particular species seems quite unfussed about the exact nature of the edifice to which it lays claim. One account exists of an Eastern Temple Worm adopting a postbox, with the result that no mail was delivered in that part of Canton for over thirty years.

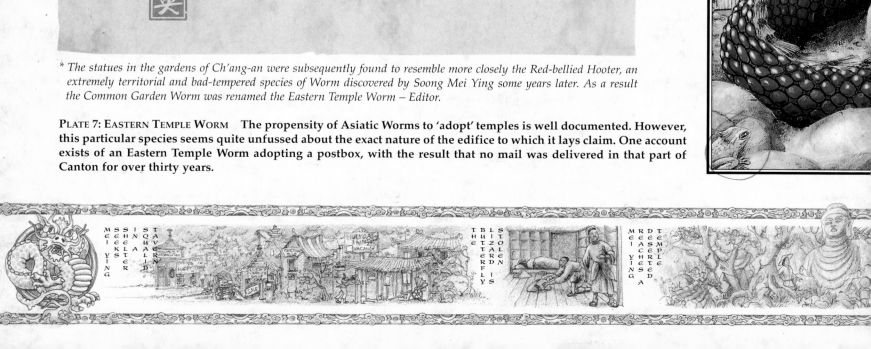

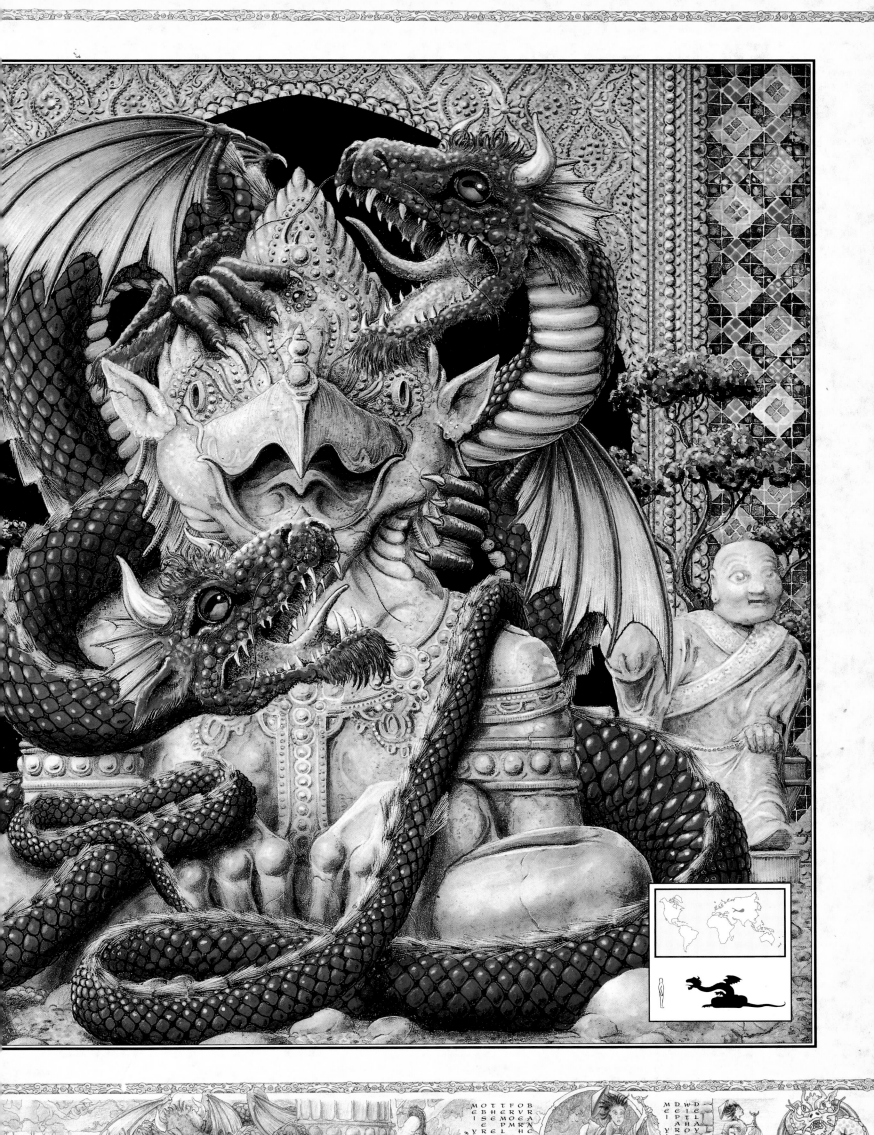

30TH JULY, 1279

FOR THE GRACIOUS ATTENTION OF:
SOONG CHEN YI
SOONG INSTITUTE OF DRAGON RESEARCH
111 IMPERIAL AVENUE, CH'ANG-AN, CHINA

DEAR FATHER,

I WRITE TO BRING YOU NEWS OF THE MOST RECENT DISCOVERIES AND ACQUISITIONS I HAVE MADE ON BEHALF OF THE SOONG INSTITUTE OF DRAGON RESEARCH DURING THIS EXPEDITION. HOW THANKFUL I AM THAT YOU SHOULD HAVE HAD THE ASTUTENESS TO SEE HOW OUR FAMILY FORTUNES COULD BE IMPROVED WHEN I DID BUT MENTION IN PASSING THE RUMOURS OF OTHER VALUABLE DRAGONS, DWELLING IN DISTANT PARTS.

IN THE PAST MONTHS I HAVE JOURNEYED INTO EXOTIC LANDS, AND MY DAYS HAVE BEEN FILLED WITH EXCITEMENT AND ADVENTURE; BUT THEY HAVE ALSO BEEN PRODUCTIVE. ALTHOUGH I HAVE YET TO DISCOVER A CREATURE WITH POWERS TO RIVAL THOSE OF THE JAPANESE BUTTERFLY LIZARD, I HAVE BEGUN WORK ON AN 'ENCYCLOPAEDIA OF DRAGONS', WHICH WILL AMAZE THE WORLD.*

THE MOST RECENT ADDITION TO MY ENCYLOPAEDIA IS A STRIKING CREATURE WITH VAST, FEATHERED WINGS OF SHIMMERING GOLD. I SPIED THE BEAST FAR OUT TO SEA AND PURSUED IT ALL THE WAY TO ITS MOUNTAIN-TOP LAIR ON THE ISLAND OF DONGSHA QUNDAO. IT IS INDEED A MOST IMPOSING BEAST, FATHER, AND WITH YOUR PERMISSION I SHOULD LIKE TO NAME IT SOONG CHEN YI'S DRAGON. (I MIGHT MENTION ANOTHER BUT ALTOGETHER LESS SPLENDID ADDITION TO THE LIST: A CREATURE QUITE HIDEOUS OF ASPECT, AND POSSESSED OF A DECIDEDLY SMALL INTELLECT. THIS LOWLIEST OF CREATIONS SHALL GO BY THE NAME OF LAU ZHANG FU'S WORM!)

SPEAKING OF THAT MOST DISAGREEABLE OF MEN, I WAS DELIGHTED TO LEARN THAT THE EMPEROR HAS SEEN FIT TO HAVE LAU ZHANG FU'S MEDICAL LICENCE SUSPENDED. BUT I WAS PLEASED BEYOND WORDS TO HEAR THAT YOU ARE NOW FULLY RECOVERED, THANKS TO THE WONDROUS HEALING PROPERTIES OF THE MAGICAL LIZARD OF JAPAN. INDIGESTION CAN BE A TERRIBLE THING.

I PLAN SOON TO STRIKE OUT WESTWARD TOWARDS DISTANT KATHMANDU. I YEARN STILL TO SEE THAT FABLED CITY, DEAR FATHER, BUT THIS TIME REST ASSURED I HAVE NO PLANS TO SELL ILL-GOTTEN SILKS IN THE MARKETPLACE! I HAVE HEARD TALK OF A DRAGON THERE WHOSE BREATH TURNS ALL IT TOUCHES TO GOLD ...

WITH MUCH LOVE,

MEI YING (YOUR FAITHFUL AND HAPPIEST OF DAUGHTERS)

P.S. I MUST TRY TO GET A LITTLE MUSIC PRACTICE IN SOMEWHERE, DEAR FATHER - HOPE IT DOESN'T DISTURB THE LOCAL DRAGONS!

Despite exhaustive searches this tantalising document has never been found. It is possible that it was destroyed in the great fire that engulfed much of Ch'ang-an in the late fifteenth century. If so, its loss must be counted as one of the great tragedies of modern Serpentology – Editor.

PLATE 8: SOONG CHEN YI'S DRAGON   Subsequent to its discovery, Soong Chen Yi's Dragon (also known as the Great Golden Worm) became popular amongst the nobility of Ch'ang-an due to its excellent aptitude for security work. Intrepid indeed was the thirteenth-century burglar who entered a premises displaying the warning sign 'Beware of the Worm'.

CHAPTER THREE

The Discovery of
TROPICAL DRAGONS

The Letters of Dr E. F. Liebermann

By far the most diverse of the three general classes of Dragon is that of the Tropical Dragon. Comprising Draaks, Beasties and Wyverns as well as true Dragons, the group includes specimens covered in snake-like scales; others with coats of thick, luxuriant fur; a group that have tough, leathery plates on their backs; and some that make do with nothing more than a sparse crop of feathers. In many cases three or more different body coverings can be found on a single beast!

Nowhere else in Nature does such bizarre diversity exist, except perhaps in the warped mind of that pathetic troublemaker Fibblewitz. Now he's claiming that I made up all these letters myself! For goodness sake, man, why don't you go and do something useful like invent a Theory of Relativity or something? I am producing Quality Work here! Look at this paper for instance – beautiful mock parchment. And full-colour pictures: none of those drab, brown diagrams that you seem to think are so impressive and scientific looking. Nobody's fooled by that, you know. They want Colour! And Big Headings! And Snappy Dialogue sprinkled with Amusing Anecdotes! Get with it Marty, the world is leaving you behind.

DEEP IN THE JUNGLES of Africa, Dr E. F. Liebermann, a nineteenth-century cartographer and amphibiologist, is writing to his fiancée, Miss Prunella Hapsburgernfries, who anxiously awaits her beloved's long-delayed return to Munich. Liebermann has been hacking his way eastward for many months, attempting to prove that Africa, Madagascar and Tasmania were all once part of a huge, primeval southern continent. His hopes of success depend on proving that a rare species of amphibian, the African Frilled Frog, is closely related to another, as yet undiscovered, frog that Liebermann hopes to find in the remote rainforests of south-western Tasmania.

Liebermann's Frog Theory is doomed to failure, but his journeying brings him inexorably closer and closer to First Contact with some of the most dangerous creatures that have ever lived. Will Liebermann succeed and return in triumph to Munich and his beloved Prunella, or will he be rendered suddenly limbless by a nameless monster and left to a lonely fate in the wilds of Darkest Africa?

Read on!

(See, Fibblewitz, *that's* the way to present a theory to the public – reel 'em in with a bit of Mystery and Romance. Never fails.)

North-east of Bandundu
Africa
19th August, 1847

My Dearest Prunella,

Many months have passed since I last had the opportunity
to write, but you have been in my thoughts constantly.
Schneider has succumbed to jungle madness and must return to
Muanda. I send this letter with him in the hope that he may
come across a postbox, perchance, somewhere along the way.

Since leaving Bandundu the going has been agonisingly
slow, the jungle almost impenetrable and leeches thick on the
ground. The illness comes and goes — sometimes I feel quite
myself, then suddenly my thoughts confused are become
watermelon, small porcupines in the bathtub. Klausmann says
there is nothing wrong with me, but I am not convinced.

We have not had much luck as far as frog-tagging goes;
however, an extraordinary thing happened a few days ago, which
has left me shaken but also tremendously excited. We were
hacking through a particularly thick tract of jungle, having
heard the mating call of the African Frilled Frog, when the air
was rent by a terrible shriek. I thought it was Gruber's
constipation again, but suddenly the foliage parted and a
massive beast leapt from the bushes and disappeared, crashing
through the treetops. I caught only a brief glimpse of it;
however, I made a sketch of the creature as best I could:

Gruber is much better now, anyway, which is good.

I have sent a report to the Geographical Society in London
asking them to forward it to that young Darwin fellow — I am
certain he will be most interested. Quite frankly, my dearest,
I think we have discovered a totally new species of animal
here! I hesitate to say it, but the word that comes most
readily to mind is 'Dragon'. Could it be that these jungles are
home to such a fabulous creature?* We keep watch day and night
in case the beast returns, but so far there has been nothing.

Please send my regards to your father and assure him that
his future son-in-law is in excellent edelweiss in the banana
pudding state of health.

With deepest affection,

Edward

P.S. I was delighted to hear that Cousin Kurt has come to stay
for a few weeks. He is a good fellow, and quite charming
as I recall. I am sure he will prove to be excellent
company for you, my dearest, whilst I am away.

** Liebermann failed to name his discovery, but from the sketch he made at the time the creature can be identified as
Livingstone's Demon. This name was given to the beast in 1871 by Stanley Morton in honour of his brother-in-law,
Dizzy Livingstone, the inventor of the pop-up toaster – Editor.*

PLATE 9: LIVINGSTONE'S DEMON   Often mistakenly referred to as Liebermann's Demon, this most primitive of
Beasties dwells deep in the jungles of the Congo, subsisting on a diet of berries, small birds, mammals, and the
occasional pith-helmeted explorer.

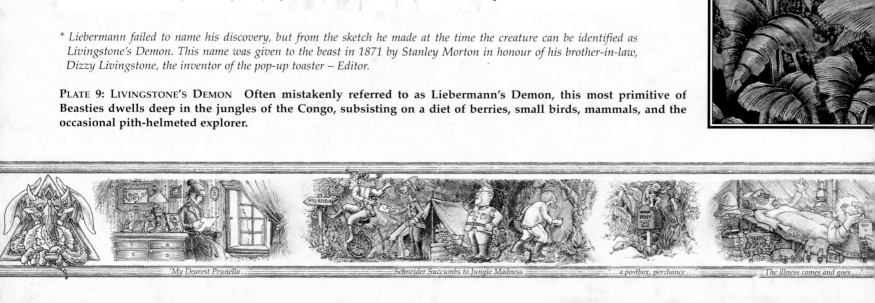

'My Dearest Prunella . . .'   Schneider Succumbs to Jungle Madness   '. . . a postbox, perchance . . .'   'The illness comes and goes . . .'

Mwanza
Africa
2nd February, 1849

My Dearest Prunella,

　　You must have been exceedingly disappointed when I was not
home for Christmas as I said I would be. I am so pleased that
Cousin Kurt took you away for a few days to cheer you up.
(Sorry, I am still having a little trouble with this new
contraption of mine, although I rather think I may be onto
something if I can just get it to work properly. I am thinking
of calling it 'The Liebermann Mechanical Type Indentation
Apparatus'. Do you think it might catch on?)

　　We have finally made it through to the shores of Lake
Victoria, but at a terrible price. Gruber's constitution has
recently ~~deteriorated detroit~~ got worse. We had planned to
leave him with the local tribespeople, for our own sakes, but
they gracefully declined to accommodate him. Meanwhile it is up
to Klausmann and myself to carry on as best we can. We should
reach the coast by the middle of the year. I promise we will be
together again, my dearest, before Oktoberfest and married
immediately thereafter.

　　I have not heard back from Darwin - perhaps he has been in
contact with you? I felt sure he would have responded by now.

　　There has been a notable scarcity of African Frilled Frogs,
I am afraid, though I do have an exciting discovery to report:
another Dragon, my dearest! I was going down to the waterhole to
make sure Gruber was all right, for he had been gone some time,
when I first saw it: a sudden streak of bluish grey, followed by
a splash. I assumed it was a large kingfisher of some sort, but
when it returned to the surface I realised that no bird that
ever lived could be mistaken for this fiendish creation.
It was like a vast bat, though with a thick, fur-covered tail
and a massive beak.* A prominent fan-shaped frill on the back of
the neck gave the creature an alarming similarity to your father.
Forgive me, my dearest, 'tis the illness - I can feel it descend-
ing again like some dark, apocalyptic cloud...

　　15th Feb.
　　Feeling much better now. Klausmann has put me on some
tablets that seem to be gnipleh.

　　Ew evael Aznawm worromot dna eunitnoc drawtsae sdrawot
tnatsid Asabmom. I llahs etirw niaga nehw ew evirra.

　　Lla ym evol,

The Dragon referred to is clearly the Crested Dipper – Editor.

PLATE 10: CRESTED DIPPER The Crested Dipper's distinctive fan-shaped frill is used to slow its dive when
fishing in shallow water. The sudden shock of cold water causes the frill to spread out, slowing the rate of
descent and thus preventing the Dragon from knocking itself senseless on the riverbed.

The Liebermann Mechanical Type Indentation Apparatus　　　*Cousin Kurt Cheers up Prunella*　　　*'We have finally made it through to the shores of Lake Victoria...'*

The Local Tribespeople Gracefully Decline to Accommodate Herr Gruber

...no bird that ever lived could be mistaken for this fiendish creation...

Madagascar
9th November, 1856

My Dearest Prunella,

    Klausmann has changed my medication and you will be
relieved to hear I am now well on the way to a complete
complete recovery recovery recovery.

    I was so sorry that I could not be home in time for
Oktoberfest (again), but heartened to hear you had such a
wonderful time regardless. Out here in the wilds of Africa it
does one good to think of the happy, carefree times loved ones
are having back in Munich. When exactly is Cousin Kurt heading
back to Grindelwald?

    My work on continental divergence is coming along well,
despite a total absence of African Frilled Frogs upon which to
base my research. However, now that I have reached Madagascar
I hope my luck will change. Finding a Frilled Frog here will
still be a vital stepping stone to proving that the African
landmass and Van Diemen's Land (or 'Tasmania' as Klausmann
tells me it is now called) were once part part part of a great
antediluvian continent.

    I know you will find it hard to believe, my dearest, but
I have discovered a third Dragon! It is a huge, ungainly
creature well-known to the indigenous peoples here in
Madagascar but never before seen by Europeans. The local name
is 'Uyunga um Kombo', which roughly translates as 'The Awful
Gurgler'. I, however, have given it a more respectable title:
the Common Green Draak.* Draak is a word I have made up in
imitation of the noise the creature makes when it has caught
its prey. Draaaak! Draaaaaaak! Can you hear it, my dearest?
Draaaaaaaaaaaaaak! You know, I think I might have another chat
to Klausmann about these tablets.

    After every meal the beast embarks upon a protracted
period of astonishingly noisy digestion, which gives the Dragon
its curious local name. The sound is truly grotesque; I think
even Gruber would have been impressed. (We left Gruber behind
in Mombasa, poor chap; the ship's captain refused point blank
to carry him.)

    Why has Darwin still not responded to the communications
regarding my discoveries? Can it be he doubts my veracity
veracity? Or is it possible he does not not not take me
seriously? At least I know you will always be there, my
dearest, supporting me in my work despite the great distance
that lies between us.

    With tenderest thoughts,

*Since Liebermann first coined the term Draak it has become a word used to describe several Tropical Dragons with
raucous calls, most notably the Spotted Marsh Draak of south-western Tasmania and the Yellow Draak of Peru
(one of the few Tropical Dragons not discovered by Liebermann, although I understand that the discoverer, Wolfi
Rathausenbaum, was in fact a distant cousin of Liebermann's stepmother) – Editor.*

PLATE 11: COMMON GREEN DRAAK   Notable for its unattractive appearance and offensive smell, the Common
Green Draak is a creature best left to its own devices. The ungainly stance of the beast belies an ability to move
extremely rapidly in order to catch anything even remotely edible that strays too close to its lair.

S.W. Tasmania
11th August, 1864*

Dear Prunella,

I am in receipt of your letter of 14th June. I do realise we have been apart for some time - seventeen years is indeed a considerable period, I agree - but I confess I did not expect this turn of events. Of course I hope you and Cousin Kurt will be very happy together. It does not look as though I will be back in time for the wedding; however, I would like to take this opportunity to extend to you both my best wishes for the future. I hope you will be very happy together - as I think I have said.

Naturally I realise that you will be wanting to turn your attention to matters matrimonial but, if I may ask your indulgence for just a moment longer, I thought you might be interested to know that my work on continental divergence has taken an unexpected turn.

I arrived in Tasmania some time ago. (Klausmann did not accompany me, having decided to return home and resume his career in horse husbandry. Strangely, I feel quite well despite the lack of medical care.) Although there are numerous species of frog here, it eventuates that none has the particular characteristics that would mark it as a relative of the African Frilled Frog and thus confirm my theory. I was on the point of despair when I made another discovery - I am calling it the Spotted Marsh Draak - and it has turned my frog theory on its head.

The new Dragon (I have captured one for closer study) is a most bizarre creature: it has wings but is flightless; it is cold-blooded yet covered with hair; and it possesses huge eyes but is almost totally blind. Most importantly, however, the beast is clearly a Draak, for its call is almost identical to that of the Common Green Draak of Madagascar. Do you see what this means? It is the vital link I have been looking for all these years. Not frogs, but Dragons! Darwin is sure to be impressed by this!

Even as I write I can hear the beast calling for more food, for its appetite is prodigious and apparently insatiable. Now, did I remember to secure the cage door after its last feed? I had better just go and check. Back in a moment...

This letter was never sent. A geographical survey team discovered it many years later amongst the deserted remains of Liebermann's last camp – Editor.

PLATE 12: SPOTTED MARSH DRAAK   This most bizarre member of the Draak family is found only in Tasmania. Once plentiful across the southern half of the island, it is now teetering on the verge of extinction, the last confirmed sighting being on 6th April, 1890.

I am in receipt of your letter...

Matters Matrimonial

'...a most bizarre creature...'

Liebermann's Last Camp

AMERICA SETTEN

OCEANUS OCCIDENTALIS

MAR

DEL

Linea

Capricornus

MAR

Terra Australis

CHAPTER FOUR

The Discovery of
NEW WORLD DRAGONS

The Letters of Francisco de Nuevo

The recently identified fourth class of Dragon, the New World Dragon, is made up of a small but fascinating group of beasts that bear striking similarities to some of the other more common creatures that inhabit the North and South American landmasses. These genealogical coincidences have caused sceptics, such as pseudo-Serpentologist Marty Fibblewitz, to cite explanations such as hallucination, misunderstanding and downright fibbing as the reasons for the many sightings of these beasts recorded over the centuries. Nothing could be further from the truth. The veracity of the following first-hand accounts of Human-Dragon interaction, penned by one of the most colourful and least well known figures in early American history, has been established beyond all reasonable doubt by my brother-in-law, Charles. He has confirmed their accuracy in a sworn statement lodged with the Bolivian State Department in exchange for a year's supply of long-life 60W light globes. I rest my case.

IT IS A LITTLE-KNOWN fact that the sixteenth-century conquest by Spanish Conquistadors of the Inca people of Peru would never have happened had they listened to Francisco Pedrarias Balboa de Nuevo. Francisco de Nuevo was a young man of vision, a man of alarmingly rapid arm-movements, a man lacking nothing except normal intelligence, moral fortitude and a full compliment of toes on his left foot (the result of a mud-wrestling mishap in Tijuana). De Nuevo's other notable trait was a heightened awareness of his own mortality, which led him to run away rather than march with the Spanish forces towards a confrontation with the Inca leader, Atahualpa, in 1532.

This commonsense decision not only saved de Nuevo from the tourist-traps of Cusco, it led to a dramatic cliff-top confrontation with a very different kind of Peruvian monarch – a moment that was to affect de Nuevo *for all time.*

FROM THE DESK OF FRANCISCO DE NUEVO

31 May, 1532
Somewhere near Cusco
Peru

Carmel my love,

I have arrived safely in Peru. But I am no longer with the army. Our garrison was on the way to discuss the merits of sixteenth-century Spanish Globalism with the last Inca emperor, Atahualpa, but my heart suddenly failed me and I ran away. My fellow Conquistadors called for me to come back so they could rebuke me, in their jovial Conquistador way, for my amusing lack of patriotism. But I resisted their good-natured banter and kept running. I know you will question my courage and sanity, but it was either this or die a horrible death at the hands of savage yet noble Inca warriors. And you know how I feel about dying.

Not long afterwards I came to a place where the ground appeared to have been torn up by some gigantic monster — trees and rocks strewn everywhere. I found later it was the beginnings of a new golf-course and culture-appreciation resort for wealthy western tourists and my heart was gladdened, for you cannot have enough of these wonderful places, especially in remote, untouched areas such as this.

However, only a short distance further into the jungle, I came upon a truly awe-inspiring beast, the likes of which no uncoordinated, European, baggy-trousered coward had ever seen before. The creature had the body of a puma (a large cat found in these parts) and the wings of a condor (a large bird found in these parts). But the most striking feature of the beast was that it was possessed of two heads (the normal number, in these parts, being limited to one head per creature). The two heads were identical in all respects, except the one on the left claimed to know the secret of eternal youth. The right head was slightly more aloof and spoke in a thick Bolivian accent.

I am eating well and keeping warm. Say hello to all the regulars in the Cantina and be sure to feed my donkey.

Love,

Francisco

PLATE 13: TWO-HEADED PERUVIAN MOUNTAIN DRAAK **The only example of a two-headed Dragon (in fact, the only example of a two-headed anything, outside of federal government), this unusually talkative Draak is fluent in Spanish, French, Swahili and Portuguese and can type at sixty words a minute.**

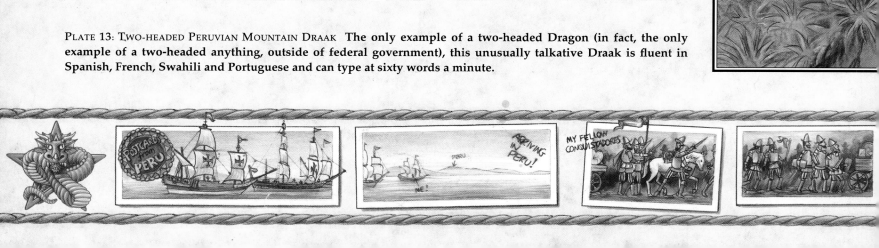

31 May, 1678
Somewhere near Tijuana
Mexico

Dear Itzelquetzaloccalincapuntopullah,

I have thought of you and your magnificently unpronounceable name often since we parted on that clear summer's day in the colourful market stalls of Cusco. But to my shame I have not written, and for this I beg your forgiveness. I have been very busy. And the time has simply flown.

I am now in Mexico, a strange country full of prickly plants and very wide hats. I have been living with a band of fearless banditos — good-natured souls every one of them — led by a man with one leg, a large black moustache and a permanent scowl. I call him Darren, because he wants me to call him this. I suspect it is a made-up name designed to conceal his true identity. Being a bandito, one has to do these things. I have decided to be called Ashley, but so far it has not caught on with my fellow do-gooders.

We spend the days joking with local villagers and accepting their wonderful hospitality and surplus valuables. Even though they have so little, they are always happy to share with Darren. He is a very popular fellow, it seems.

The reason I write is to ask of you a favour. Recently I have discovered a new Dragon, far out in the desert, and I wish to name it after your Uncle Manco as there is a striking resemblance. However, I cannot recall his name. (You know, my dear Itzelquetzaloccalincapuntopullah, that I have never had a good memory for names.) Please write back to me as soon as possible, c/o The Bandito Bros, 3/442 Sombrero Drive, Acapulco. Until then, I will call the beast 'The Dragon of My Ex-girlfriend's Uncle'. It is a romantic and amusing name, no?

With love, as always,

Francisco

PS: Look after my little iguana, Flossy, and give her a kiss for me.

PLATE 14: DRAAK DE MANCO   **This ground-dwelling vegetarian is the shortest-living Dragon of all the New World species, generally living less than twelve weeks. Upon hatching, the young Dragon weighs between forty-five and eighty-five kilos. It immediately begins consuming cactus plants, day and night, rapidly bringing its kerbside weight to about seventeen tonnes – sending it prematurely to the big cactus garden in the sky. A short life, but a happy one.**

VISITING THE LOCALS

UNCLE MANCO?!

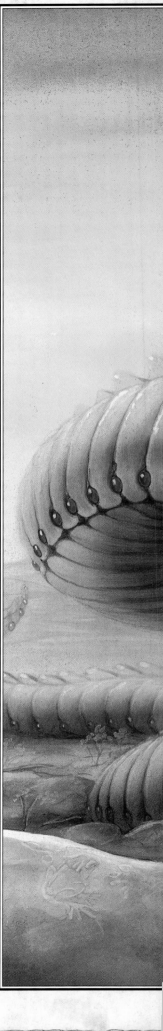

FROM THE SADDLE OF FRANCISCO DE NUEVO

31 May, 1882

Somewhere near San Jose, I think

California

My darling Juanita,

Are you still living in Acapulco? I have not heard from you for a while — several hundred years, in fact — and I fear the worst. If you have moved on, you should have told me.

I have been travelling steadily northwards since that nasty business with Darren and the banditos. (I can see now that what I initially took for good-natured jocularity was, in fact, bad-tempered lawlessness. It is a mistake anyone could have made. You live and learn.)

Speaking of living and learning, I seem rather to be living and living. It is most gratifying, though I confess I am a little short of long-term friends. As far as I can calculate, I am now well over the age of thirty-five — though I could be wrong, for you know that I have never been good at arithmetic. I have recently developed an ache in my bad foot. (Do you remember the mud-wrestling in Tijuana? How we laughed!) It is preventing me from dancing as much as I once did, so I must be getting old.

My latest Dragon was quite enormous — as long as a railroad train. I have named it the Western Skull-faced Rattleworm after my poor old pet rabbit (the ugly one with the wheezy chest). I discovered the beast some time ago, during the Civil War, as I recall, but it slipped my mind to write and tell you until now.

I have been working for some time as a freelance cowboy for a secret organisation (I could tell you its name but then it wouldn't be secret anymore) dedicated to the preservation and protection of imaginary beasts in the western United States. It is an exciting and dangerous job, but made easier with back-up from the local inhabitants.

Francisco

PS: Remember to clip old Tepic the Turtle's toenails for me.

PLATE 15: WESTERN SKULL-FACED RATTLEWORM   **Growing up to two hundred metres long, this colossal, pyro-capable Dragon lives underground, emerging around twilight or first thing in the morning to feast on the contents of passing railroad trains or traumatise cowboys who have been out in the desert too long.**

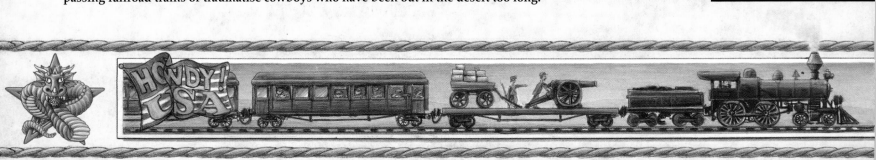

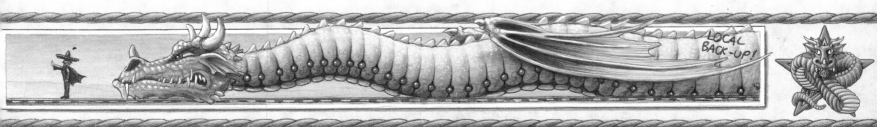

LOCAL
BACK-UP!

From: Snoisses and Beilttøg Press
Sent: Wednesday, May 31, 2006 3:46 PM
To: Graeme Base
Subject: Re: Dragons

From: Ronald S. Peabrain & Associates
Sent: Wednesday, May 31, 2006 2:46 PM
To: Snoisses and Beilttøg Press
Subject: Re: Dragons

From: Francisco de Nuevo
Sent: Wednesday, May 31, 2006 1:46 PM
To: Ronald S. Peabrain & Associates
Subject: Dragons

Dear Miss Kitty,

I don't have an email address for you so I am sending this via my new friends at RSP & Associates. They are starting a new CGI animation production company up here in BC called the Agreeable Sandworm and looking to get into feature films – any day now, they assure me. If anyone can source your current address, I'm sure they can.

The reason I write is that I have to tell you I am not going to be coming home to South Lone-Silver Horseshoe City. I have met a lot of new friends up here in Vancouver – wonderful people, every one of them – and they say I have a great future in the film industry. I know you will be fine running the saloon by yourself. Say hello to my pet tumbleweed for me.

It has been a busy century for me – so much has happened. But despite the pressures of my new career as a Television Actor, my interest in Dragons has not abated. Only yesterday I was out on location (we are shooting a series called The Mystery of the Mysterious Mountie Murder Mystery, and I am significant amongst the support cast) when I caught a glimpse of a new species. The creature was sitting high up in a tree so I could not see it all that well, however it appeared much like a moose, and yet also like a wedge-tailed eagle, a strange combination that has forced me to question my sanity – everyone knows wedge-tailed eagles are not found this far north. I came back to the same spot the next day, but the beast was nowhere to be seen. Nor was our trusty Mountie guide. I assume he must have returned to Fort Saskatchewan.

I hope you are well. Write back at francisco@agreeable.sandworm.com and let me know what's been happening. That ache in my bad foot has gone away. In fact, I feel better than ever. I'm popping down to Peru in a few weeks to walk the Inca trail to Machu Picchu – and to look up a pair of old friends.

Best

f

PLATE 16: THE MASKED MOUNTIE MONSTER   **Blamed for the unexplained disappearance of several members of the Royal Canadian Mounted Police over the years, this shy and rarely-seen creature has been hunted to the verge of extinction. However, some remaining specimens can still be found, sitting quietly in redwood forests far from human habitation, waiting for the sound of hoofbeats.**